fast forward

Published by FF>> Press.

ISBN: 978-0-9817852-0-2

Library of Congress Control Number: 2008929360

Cover photo courtesy Stacy Walsh.
Graphic design/layout by Nicholas Michael Ravnikar.

fast forward

A Collection of Flash Fiction

Volume 1

Edited by

K. Scott Forman
Kona Morris
Nancy Stohlman

FF>> Press, 2008

Contents

To the Reader >>>

At FF>>, we believe we have the answer for your perpetually diminishing attention span: a story under 1,000 words. We understand that your daily planner is filled with appointments, your to-do list is jammed, and it can be difficult to commit to reading something that would take more than a couple pages to finish. That is why we have pooled our talents with the aim of saving the experience of literature for you. Yes, you.

The succinct energy of flash fiction is a walk down the driveway to get the mail, a mischievous smile between strangers, the story that you almost remember as you go to sleep at night. We are presenting stories from 20 writers with wildly different styles, each exploring the genre of flash fiction.

FF>> began as an experiment in long-distance, electronic collaboration among students in the low-residency MFA program at Naropa University's Jack Kerouac School of Disembodied Poetics. While the press was enabled by our mutual enrollment at Naropa, many of us have never met in person.

Our goal is to publish a collection of flash fiction each year. To find more information about how to submit, order future publications, and collaborate with us on this project, please visit our website, the address for which appears on the "Acknowledgments" page of this volume.

Cheers,
FF>>

Leah Rogin-Roper, Nicholas Michael Ravnikar, Kona Morris, Elizabeth Keicher, K. Scott Forman, Nancy Stohlman, Dawn Sueoka, Stacy Walsh, Justin M. Kulyk, Kaen Joyler, and Megan Burns

Andrew Wille
Electricity

The chair is dark, varnished oak. Its wide seat and tall back are padded with thick leather cushions.

Dr. Westwell pinches his nose. He wonders if future societies will eliminate such violent acts entirely. While these rituals remain constitutional, perhaps his revolutionary technology can make the ordeal more humane, more efficient.

He's come far. Early trials caused rats to explode. Cats kept their bodily forms but not their bodily functions, and the smell would not be tolerated by paying spectators. By the time he was experimenting with orang-utans, lavatorial habits were not a problem.

The copper wires are coated with green rubber and curl away to the aluminium control panel. The fingers on its many dials rest at zero, and the filaments in the glass dome above the chair are dim.

The public gallery is filling. Ladies unveil grave faces, gentlemen unfold opera glasses.

A grey-coated attendant holds open the door of the waiting chamber. "Dr. Westwell, the subject is ready."

The doctor nods sombrely, massaging his earlobe. The subject is led by the hand across the shiny black tiles. Still moist from the showers, he is a suitably handsome specimen, tall, dark-haired, and broad-shouldered. He wears only a blindfold. Tests on clothed chimps had failed; for the procedure to be executed, the subject must be naked.

A woman in the front row borrows her husband's opera glasses. He snatches them back.

The subject is placed in the chair. It tilts back. His legs splay open. His hands dangle across his hammy thighs until the attendant buckles leather straps around his wrists and ankles, ties thick rope above his knees and across his chest, and fastens a hefty collar around his neck. The subject grins. Doping makes this process kinder, less humiliating, but Dr. Westwell notes he should use a drug with a more sobering effect next time. Grinning is not appropriate for such solemn occasions.

The doctor lowers the copper helmet on to the subject's head. A very coronation, with Dr. Westwell as kingmaker. He folds the flaps over the subject's ears, then turns the knob on its top through one, two, three clicks that echo round the laboratory.

Slow down, slow down. The doctor inhales, exhales. He strides along the control panel, pressing each button, tugging every lever. His heels tap on the tiles, fingers on the dials twitch. He pulls the penultimate switch, and the dome flickers with a pink glow.

Murmurs rise from the gallery as the other subject appears on the large overhead screen. Shiny black tiles, curly green wires, a chair of oak and leather and buckled straps: her chamber is identical, except it is on the other side of the world. She is also dark-haired, and her naked skin glistens, and she wears a copper helmet and a blindfold, and she smiles. The attendant beside her gives a thumbs-up.

Dr. Westwell rests his palm over the great white switch at the heart of the controls. A bead of perspiration drips off the end of his nose, and he wipes it away with a starched cotton handkerchief. He pulls the switch.

The pink glow grows warmer, fills the room with soft dawn light, now orange, now mauve. The male subject stretches back in his chair, the light throbs faster and harder, and thousands of miles away his respondent stretches too. Both lick their lips, roll their tongues back in, smirk.

Their motions are controlled in unison: a tilt of the head, a push against a leather strap, the digging of heels into footrests. Then heads are rocking, hips are bucking. Whispers and groans rise to the gallery, where curious faces crane forward, bathed in violet.

Dr. Westwell stands back, fingers his lips. The operation to transport sexual impulse is a success. A way of reaching long-distance loved ones, a means to manage reproduction, a system of eradicating disease and managing overpopulation: his cure for fornication is the race's salvation.

The light turns red.

Barbara Henning
Biology >>

Upon catching me in the outside hallway dressed in my pink slip, Frankie slapped me with the front of his hand and then with the back. It was his only defense. When he had left for work, I was rooted for the time being, asleep in our bed, naked.

Unexpectedly, he came home on his lunch break.

I was wondering where you were, he thundered. Now I know.

I held my fingers under my swollen belly, holding up the frantic weight of the baby, turning and twisting. I was huddled into the corner.

Frankie, I said, weeping, you hurt me.

He was breaking everything in the baby's room. I heard the crib hit the wall. He was crying. You fucking whore.

I stood still in the hallway for thirty seconds, frozen in his gaze. When he started coming toward me, though, I slapped him first. We had never struck each other before.

You weren't paying any attention to me. You were coming home so late.

Roots serve as an anchor and a passage to absorb water and minerals.

You were fucking that asshole next door.

He started for the door.

I heard the back door slam. My lover ran out the back door. In a railroad apartment, between the front and back door, one room opens up into the other.

If a stem or shoot tip is cut off, the supply of hormones is disrupted and one or more buds will usually begin to grow, forming a new shoot which in turn will inhibit the development of others.

I was washing the dishes when he first rang the bell.

We began to talk about botany and the elm trees on Alter Road.

Plants produce seeds enclosed in an ovary, he said with his deep voice. He was a student at the university. He showed me his collections of leaves and talked about the forests in the upper peninsula. He went on about the way trees cross-pollinate when the wind and the birds take the seeds.

My legs were swollen. I was heavy and overdue.

We sat on the porch under the shade of an elm tree in early spring. Everything was in bloom. The elms in this city are infected with a deadly fungus in the sap of the tree. It spreads from one to the next. Virus is Latin for poison. The heartwood of every tree is dead. Nevertheless, each year a new ring forms.

He was home studying in the daytime.

His skin was rosy.

He was tall and lanky.

Like a conspicuous flower, he said. The aim is to attract an insect or some other animal. Something new comes into being by modifying that which already exists.

The first night after I met him, he cooked me vegetables and rice.

Between want and plenty. My skin was burning

hot. He pullèd up my negligee and held his hands on my swollen belly. I was wet with pregnant desire. He pulled me over his face, pushing his hands against my breasts, heavy and wet. I thought he would climb up inside me, beside the baby turning in my womb.

He is the father, he said, but I am the farmer.

In the order necessarily created by man, the elm is part of the kingdom of Plantae, the division of Anthophyta, the class of Dicotyledonae, the order of Urticales, the family of Ulmaceae, the genus of Ulmus, the species of Ulmus americana L., according to Linnaeus.

I folded the slip into the suitcase with the others. The spring rain stripped the pollen from the trees. Fragments of seeds and petals were scattered over the sidewalk. I stepped over some petals and into the taxi. I was running a fever. On my way to the hospital, I was wearing low heels and a shawl.

Megan Burns
Water Song >>

A woman is standing on her dining room table. Her skin, the color of caramel, sticks to her infant son's naked chest. His head rests on the soft part of her breast just beneath the collar bone and beads of sweat pool in the crevices where their bodies meet. He sleeps beneath the hot breath of her frantic exhalations and to the sound of her rapid heartbeat. His small hands rest on the outside of her arms, ten limp fingers twitching occasionally. Her arms encircle him, one curving around his lower back above his diaper and one curling higher so that her palm cups his bony shoulder closer and closer while she hums a lullaby whose words have disappeared.

It is impossible to make out what lies beneath her elbows. The water swallows the ends of the boy's fat-ringed legs and his mother's body below the waist. Oil slicks swirl on the surface in rainbow patterns as the water moves in through broken window panes and door slats, not as fast as when it first began but still not stopping. Water laps the walls where family photographs still hang, half submerged. Several chairs from another room float by and something heavy hits the back of her knees threatening to push them from their perch. The water reeks of garbage and sewage and food rotting in the hundred plus August heat. Screams pierce the silence beyond the walls, increasing in pitch and then disappearing. As the water rises, she loosens one arm to grab the ceiling. She whispers into his tiny ear secrets that the water keeps.

Elizabeth Keicher
Reflections >>

I'm watching you, your reflection in the window. It's pitch black outside and the lights in our sitting room make the window seem like a mirror. You are reading the newspaper, effortlessly, in the far end of the room. You have on shorts, even though it's snowing outside. I have an unopened book on my lap that's been that way for hours. The comforter from our bed is holding me tight, and I am clutching a pair of tiny baby booties in my right hand. I have been looking at you in the window for what seems like an eternity.

The phone rings for the thousandth time. I reach over and pick up the receiver and form the word hello. Only the second part comes out; my throat is too dry to form the first part. It's your mother calling for the second time this afternoon. How are we? Should she come over? Will we come over for dinner? I tell her no, again, and force a smile as I reply so she hears it in my voice and won't call again. I look back at the window, at your reflection.

As I hang up the phone I wipe the moisture from my cheek, and catch your eye in the window. I'm sure looking at me makes you think of him or her so I look away ashamed, knowing after eleven weeks I failed all of us.

I move the tiny light yellow booties from my right hand to my left. They are one of the few things we had purchased so early, after deciding to paint the spare room a similar yellow. The cotton is so soft, almost silk like. I have been clutching them for the past three days. Holding them for dear life.

The doorbell rings. You fold up the last section of the newspaper and head past me, eyes to the floor. At the door I hear the sweet sound of my mother's voice, brimming with sadness and weighed down with pity. And I hear you, quietly lowering your voice as you shuffle my mother in.

Walking in the room, you remind me that my mother has brought food, and will stay to eat with us. I hear you, but on delay, and by the time I look up at you, you are looking at the floor. I wonder if you blame me. You take the book off my lap, and pick up the slew of tissues surrounding me. Leaning over, you push the blanket off my shoulders, and for a second, I believe you'll graze my forehead with a kiss. I close my eyes in anticipation but after a moment I realize I am wrong.

Instead, you reach down and take my elbow, helping me up from the couch. As I stand, one of the booties slips from my clutch. Before I can pick it up, your gaze falls to it. I don't know what to say, and warm tears stream down my face. For the first time in days I look at you directly. You reach down for the bootie, but hold my gaze as you pick it up. You tell me it's okay; you know it was an accident, and hand me the bootie.

"We could play a game of calcetto—two on two."

"No, that won't do, there's five of us."

"One of us can be goalie."

"No, let's do something else besides soccer."

"Yeah, that's all we've done this week and my knees hurt."

It's true, that's all we have done for a week. Mario's knees are scabbed and when he runs they break off, the blood rolls down his leg and looks gross. No, soccer won't do today. Salvatore dribbles the ball from foot to foot without letting it touch the ground, counting as he kicks the ball.

"Then what are we going to do?" I'm bored, very bored. Guido counts along with Salvatore, nodding his head each time Salvatore makes a count.

"Let's ride the country road to the top and race down the asphalt hill."

"No, we can't," Edgidio says. "My bike has a flat and I don't feel like fixing it."

"Then what are we going to do? I can't stand this."

"Forty-seven!" yells Salvatore.

"That wasn't forty-seven, that was forty-two," says Guido.

"No it wasn't. It was forty-seven."

"I was counting with you and you only made it to forty-two."

"You miscounted then. I counted forty-seven."

"I know what we can do—we can climb the wall and watch la puttana get it on with her boyfriend."

"No, she's not getting it on with him anymore," Salvatore says. "Besides, she hasn't been getting it on for a while now."

"Che pacchio, what a honey la puttana," says Mario who keeps picking at his scab.

"Why don't we hang out at your place, Aldo? You've got tons of things to play with," Edgidio says.

"No, I don't feel like playing at my house. My mother doesn't want us upstairs on a nice day, anyway."

"It is a nice day," agrees Mario.

"Yeah, it is a nice day," echoes Edgidio.

"It was only forty-two," Guido says.

"Forty-seven. I know what we can do, let's ring the intercom and call out spazadura. Has anyone seen the trash man today?"

"No, and he usually comes on Wednesdays."

"Yeah, let's do spazadura," says Mario.

"Okay, but this time, don't ring my mother's bell." Last time Edgidio's mother waited an entire five minutes for the garbage man, holding three loads of garbage.
I love spazadura. It's my favorite prank. At the intercom I'm giddy with excitement.

"Alright, I'll yell spazadura. Just one of us needs to yell it or they'll get suspicious, and I have the deepest voice."

We all agree. Salvatore stands to the side while we count to three and each of us smack the twenty-something buttons on the intercom and step back.

"SPAZADUUUURA!"

Immediately voices begin to answer our call so Salvatore yells out once more, "SPAZADUUUURA!" We all race to a hiding spot across the street where we can't be seen and where we can watch the main entrance.

"That was great, Salvatore," I say.

"Yeah, that was real good," says Mario whose scab is oozing blood, once again.

"Forty-two," says Guido.

"No! It was forty-seven. The last one counts."

"No it doesn't."

"Look. Look," I say.

At the entrance there are seven perplexed women holding full plastic bags looking for the garbage man. They're confused and look around, then three more women and then five.

"Who rang my buzzer?"

Edgidio's mother pushes her way to the front holding the most amount of garbage in her hands.

"God, you guys got a lot of garbage," Mario says.

We decide to crawl to the end of the building and hide ourselves in the woods. After all, Edgidio's mother might be there for a while. The best part is, before long, the real garbage man will show up and no one will come down.

"Forty-two."

"Forty-seven."

Stacy Walsh
Just One Question >>

Tess sat on the bleachers after track practice waiting for her mom to pick her up. She looked past the track to the baseball field. She thought back to the summer afternoons spent watching the Tigers on television with her grandfather and brothers. If the Tigers were losing, which was often, he would yell every word Tess was not allowed to say at the television. If the game became hopeless, he would wheel out the video game cart, and they would spend the rest of the afternoon playing Atari. Tess always wished for a hopeless game so they could play Frogger or River Raid. She stopped thinking about her grandfather when she felt her eyes well up.

Her mother pulled up in the mini-van. They rode in silence, the late-afternoon sun filtering through the windshield. Her mom had been quiet since her grandfather's funeral the previous week, barely speaking to Tess or her brothers. She'd thought her mom would cry more.

Tess noticed the tulips were beginning to unfold from the ground.

"I need to ask you something," her mom blurted out.

Normally, if her mom had a question she just asked it. Tess's mind raced as she tried to recall any recent, troublesome activity. She'd been going through all the regular motions. Good grades, extracurricular activities, no detention, chores. Tess and her brothers were trying extra hard at home and school, so as not to cause any hassle. They didn't know any other way to make their mother feel better.

"Well?" Tess ventured nervously.

"Has ... um, has anyone ever ... well, shoot," her mom stopped. She rotated her hands forward and backwards on the steering wheel as though she was wringing a washcloth.

Tess felt her stomach tighten. It was the same feeling she had at the beginning of a race. She looked straight ahead at the curving road and waited.

"Has anyone ever done anything bad to you, or, uh ... touched you in a bad way?"

Tess felt the air rush out of her lungs. Something in her brain burst and flooded her head. Before she even realized it, she was crying.

Tess saw her mom's knuckles turn white as she gripped the wheel. She couldn't imagine why her mother would ask this. How did she know?

"Oh my god," her mom whispered.

The van swerved to the right into a church parking lot. Tess couldn't stop the tears, couldn't find her voice. She never thought anyone would find out what happened in that room seven years ago. Tess stole a glance at her mom. There wasn't a discernible emotion showing. Her hands hadn't moved from the wheel. She sat looking straight ahead, unable to look at Tess.

"Who?" her mom whispered.

Her mother must know the answer to this question, if she was asking. Tess felt like she was going to be in trouble. It was one of the reasons she had never said anything.

"It was Leslie," she stated as though it was the most obvious thing in the world. There continued to be no eye contact between them. Tess took short breaths and looked out the window. A mother and two small children were in the large field next to the church flying a kite.

"Leslie? Your sister?" her mom asked in confusion. "Are you sure?"

"Yes," Tess sniffled. "I'm sure."

Like she could forget. It was a blessing Leslie moved out when Tess was eight. The nightmares stopped shortly after.

"No one else?" her mom dug one more time.

"No! Mom, who did you think it was?" she asked.

Her mom sat in silence for several seconds before rushing through her words.

"Someone's accused your father. I ... I had to ask," her mom apologized tearfully.

Tess crumpled forward in her seat as though she had been struck.

"Mom, no!" she gasped for air. "Who said that?"

Her mom turned and looked at her.

"Leslie did."

Justin M. Kulyk
The Collegian >>

Mabel Tindle's son bent over lifting one end of a futon, as her husband strained to carry the other end. She wrung her hands as she followed them tentatively, hardly hearing herself say, "Careful, Frank ... Careful."

"I've got it, Mabel—now just hush. I'm fine." Her husband's arms were shaking beneath the weight. She knew she couldn't talk him out of anything.

After they placed the futon in the U-Haul truck, Jason stood looking at his mother with a proud smile. He can hardly contain his glee, Mabel thought. Mabel dreaded this day. He looked like a man-child standing there in his skinny jeans, with his tweed jacket and his tie sitting crookedly on his chest in a fat knot. Everything he did made her upset. Time after time she had promised not to give in, to quit worrying, but she couldn't stop. Where did I go wrong with that kid? At least he's going to college. It could have been worse.

"Now what type of friends do you expect to meet with that peach fuzz sprouting from your lip?" Mabel chided.

"The kind of friends that smoke pot and drink whiskey," Jason said levelly.

"I tell you what—I'm not sending you to college to smoke pot and become a drunk. I've seen those TV shows, and don't you think I don't know what goes on there," Mabel said.

"Why do you let him get to you, Mabel?" Frank

said wearing his look of disgust, a look Mabel was all too familiar with. She never forgot that same look about a year ago when she decided to wear something "lacy" to bed.

"I know you and Dad are going to get along just great without me," Jason said.

This statement froze Mabel. Jason being the third and final child they'd seen off, she didn't know what she was going to do in the house with just herself and Frank. It had been twenty-three years since an empty home.

"Come here, Jason ... come here," Mabel wound her hand.

Jason took two steps forward and let his mother hug him. It had been over a year since she had hugged anyone. Over Jason's shoulder she looked at Frank. He was looking away. Typical, she thought and sighed. She held the embrace longer in hopes Jason would relent and wrap his arms around her, but they just hung at his sides. She backed away and surveyed him.

Jason turned to his father. They looked at each other a moment. She twisted her ring and had a tremendous urge to throw it at Frank. The look between father and son was empty, almost as empty as the look Frank gave Mabel every moment of every day. Frank only changed his expression just before dinner. Mabel recalled Jason yelling the other night, "All you care about is food, Dad! You don't care about Mom, or anyone! Just you and your goddamn food!"

It was true. There had been over five years without any act of affection from Frank. As the lingering moment spread over the two last men in her life, it dawned on her that maybe she left the stove on. She turned to look at the house.

"Oh, wait!" she exclaimed snapping father and son out of their stares. "I forgot. I have something for you, Jason. Just hold on one moment." She pointed to the house and moved in a fast walk inside. She went to the stove—it was off. She then frantically searched the kitchen for something, anything, to bring out to her son. She grabbed the first thing that leapt out at her. It was Frank's blue coffee thermos.

She walked back outside holding the thermos out in front of her with a prideful grin. Frank was astonished.

"You're giving him my thermos?" Frank protested.

"You just be quiet. He's your son, for godsakes. He needs a thermos in college. You know how Jason likes his coffee."

Jason took it without a "thanks." He just shook his head at her. Frank looked at him as he said, "Well—I guess this is it."

"This isn't it," Mabel said. "You'll be sure to come back for the holidays."

"Yeah. Why don't I just drive back in my imaginary car?" Jason scoffed. "Bye." He climbed behind the wheel. He started the truck and rolled down his window. "Dad," he said looking hard at him. "Catch!" he tossed the thermos, and Frank fumbled it. Mable's ring finally came off into her hand. She dropped it into her apron pocket and watched the truck turn out of sight.

Kaen Joyler
Joie de Vivre »

I spent all morning in the kitchen, while you were out front washing the car, so it had to rain. By the time people got settled with drinks on the patio, it began, and we hurried to move coolers and grill into the carport. Perfect timing though for me to burn the meringue pie. Forty years of cooking, since I was ten in Mother's kitchen, and I still burn dessert. Dear, that's not why I cried when everybody left, and now that I've washed my face, I feel much better.

The only time I ever saw my mother burn anything, she burned the pot roast. We lived back East then and the tv ran day and night, my father glued to the fortunes of the Mets and Knicks and Rangers. He called my mother into the front room when the news came on the black and white, something about Cuba and the Soviets. That was nineteen sixty-two. I was eight.

We didn't have an oven timer; Mother didn't need one. I was just learning to help out, cutting crisp celery stalks into little green moon wedges as I kept one eye on my father hunched forward on the sofa, mother stiff on the arm, wiping her hands on her apron. It must have been my father who noticed the smoke first. I heard him say, Good Lord, Catherine. That's when I turned to the oven and saw the wisps curling out the way hair on my nape always came loose from my ponytail.

Mother rushed in, threw open the oven door. Waved a towel she'd snatched off the counter at the black cloud that rolled out. She dumped what was left of the roast into a paper grocery bag. Folded down the top and stood there for a moment. Like she didn't quite know where this had come from and didn't quite know what to do with it. As if what she'd just pulled from the oven wasn't even remotely related to what she'd put in. She sent me to the corner market for sandwich bread and cold cuts. When I came back, the apartment was dark. Mother said they weren't hungry and sent me into the kitchen to make myself a sandwich. I picked the bag out of the trash, dumped the roast on the table. I thought if I cut off the burned part, my parents would find their appetite. The inside was gray and dry, still smoking, like the bottom of a dirty glass ashtray. Years later, seeing pictures of the war, I remembered that roast wrapped up tight in a paper bag.

I know. Just a barbeque for friends, their children keeping our children occupied. I can only figure it was the suddenness of the storm that took my mind off the oven. Didn't I fix it? Put some leftover strawberries from the fruit salad nicely around the top. Not that anyone noticed once we started on the liquor. When's the last time we turned down the lights in the living room and danced in our socks?

With the curtains open, I could see the glow of the power plant, where so many of us work, reflected in the rain clouds. The lights of a mad scientist's castle, his tower-top laboratory faking moonshine in our dark peasant night. I felt something happening out there, something that could change everything for good. I could smell the roast burning, and knew this time I couldn't just go to the corner store for something else. I had to make do. So I danced harder, like the Indians dancing the Ghost Dance. I was dancing for our children, to bring back the world before the bomb. When did you notice the pie fight? I'd fallen into a trance. None of us noticed the children running through the house (something we would never have done in our own parents' homes) with handfuls of burnt meringue, smearing it all over each other until that shrieking child signaled the game had gone too far. All that's left is the burnt-out, graham-cracker crust.

It was then, as our friends began wiping off their children, wetting dishtowels and looking around for a mop, broom, dustpan, offering to help me with the mess, apologizing—all of us embarrassed by something we'd let get out of hand—it was then I felt helpless and not just a little responsible. I think I understand my parents' loss of appetite. And sometimes I burn dinner, don't I.

As everyone started collecting their jackets, stuffing diapers in bags and putting on shoes, I stood by the door not wanting anyone to leave. That's why I started crying, as I hugged everyone, saying over and over as they got in their cars and headed off, No, it's no trouble, there'll be time enough in the morning to clean it all up.

Linh Dinh
Sleeping Together >>

The houses are strangely narrow here, hardly wide enough for a double bed, yet the population quadruples after each severe rainstorm, drizzle or just a prickling mist on a Winter morning. Don't look on the ground, ladies and gentlemen, or you might see an extremely crude version of yourself. You must trust me on this, OK? As I was saying, in a country with few private rooms, where people live on top of each other, lies and half-truths become the only forms of privacy. Lying, they assume everyone else is a liar. Those who don't lie must be either a saint or an idiot, or just plain rude. In this shimmering world of big and small deceits, people tend to become spies just to get at the impossible truth. There is an instructive story of a poor man who won a lottery. He moved his family into a mansion where each of his 13 children could have his or her own room at last. For the first time, they could think in silence and examine their firm or flabby flesh in a full-length mirror. They could hear the creaks and hums of their own brains, feel the drafts of strange doors being opened. The oldest boy realized he had a flat chest, a beer belly and no muscles. The oldest girl discovered a condor-shaped birthmark spanning her behind. After a month of daydreaming, reading, masturbating, and an unbearable loneliness bordering on madness, they decided to all sleep in the same room again.

Nancy Stohlman
An Inventory of Things >>
in My Mother's Boxes

The boxes have come every few months for over
a decade: three-pack of assorted corn relishes one pair
flannel Bugs Bunny boxers too big for my husband one
pencil with dancing skeleton on the end one ball of
rubber bands one plastic AT&T sippy bottle filled with
hard candies one yellow sequined beret one Ziploc bag
full of dried apple slices one pair green plastic sandals
too small seven bottles of shampoo and conditioner
half-used one kid's pink Minnie Mouse sweatshirt (I
have two sons) one chocolate bar almost gray with age
three homemade cassette tapes of Dalai Lama's "The
Art of Happiness" one laminated wallet-sized rendition
of "The Lord's Prayer" bag of travel sized soaps and
toothbrushes one half full bottle of Summer's Morning
essential oil one cross stitch picture with saying "A
Family is the Place Where You Always Belong" one
pile of yard sale clothes for my kids wrong sizes one
bag of dried potpourri two Tupperware bins full of
maxi pads and tampons one sparkly dress with thrift
store tag two sizes too big several loose hair combs
and ponytail holders bag of half-used nail polishes box
full of clown props: red noses honking horns squirting
pack of cigarettes oversized rubber shoes oversized
green and white polka dotted tie oversized sunglasses
orange curly wig one bag of homemade pumpkin seeds

---

one package of dry enchilada sauce one Danielle Steele book I would never read one pair of the world's softest socks cherry red one 5x7 photograph of her with her cheeks puffed up like a chipmunk one bunch of plastic daisies three photographs of her latest painting two pairs of lacy underwear too small one Santa Claus doll with cowboy hat that sings honky tonk when you press the button (sent in September) one diamond ring that was a gift from my dad when they were first married (they're divorced) one hand-knitted sweater for my son that belonged to my brother thirty years ago one "Countdown to Christmas" calendar with cocker spaniel puppies one pair grandma sunglasses one bag of old dishtowels and placemats one folder full of Martha Stewart recipes ripped from a magazine half a dozen packages of Pansy seeds Red Poppy seeds one sheet of panda bear stickers bag of deer jerky bag of pineapple jerky bag of watermelon jerky bag of turkey jerky (she just got a food dehydrator).

"Do you get them too?" I once asked my brother. "Oh yeah, I get them, too," he said, "I finally had to tell her to stop sending me her junk."

When I was a child my mother mowed the lawn in zig-zags and mandala patterns. She held impromptu funerals for potatoes that fell through the grill and perished on the coals. She gathered duck feathers around the lake and made wreaths. She started a folk band, a clown troupe; she painted my bedroom in peach and mint green stripes and made my red taffeta prom dress on her old sewing machine. She drew caricatures on hard-boiled eggs with Sharpies and returned them to the refrigerator, to my lunch boxes. She taught me that there is no other kind of life but the one that gurgles up from the pit of your belly.

I go to the thrift store every few months with boxes full of donations. My husband thinks I'm crazy for not telling her the truth. But the truth is, I'm afraid I would miss them.

Kona Morris
Sell-out Matt >>>

   Tall-legged, long-faced, slim-boned Matthew Garretty rolled into himself in a post-pubescent delayed-adolescent whirlwind engaging dance some eight years ago today. He grew up in the catastrophic absurdity of a religious mama who turned from tweaker trash to jehovahistic judger upon the knock knock knock of a witness at her door twenty-seven springs ago while Matt was still hitching a ride on her uterus. She was desperate, battered, ankle swollen and pregnant, and something about the perfectly pitched line or the prodigious promise struck some deep integral part inside of her that would incite a lifetime of prayer and devotion.

   He grew up poor and white in Missouri without birthdays, balloons, pumpkins or presents. He grew up estranged from mainstream american youthfulness, catching glimpses of it through the perpetual doorway on the other side of his mother's eager fanaticism. Little bright eyes blinking away the baptized boundaries of his life. Nintendo dreams and easter bunny fantasies slid like pale rumors across the mat of his childhood.

   At eighteen, after accidenting upon the treasure of a library Twain, the awkwardly tall and thin-faced teenaged Matthew decided he wanted to break the fast of his jehovah mission to go get a collegiate education.

He wasn't trying to betroth another worldview, but rather indulging in a subliminal attempt at normality through his organic desire to educate himself. His mom and newly acquired stepfather, along with the entire Kingdom Hall community, did not approve of this plan.

They told Matthew that the only school he should go to was the one that would further train him for door to door soul saving and paradise praying and that a public university would only introduce evil thoughts and false histories. His mother and step authority threatened to take away their parental bond if he did not comply with their wishes. And that marked the first time in Matt's life that he formed a strong opinion about his home life.

He said goodbye to his bare-walled bedroom one exasperated summer night and crawled out the rusty side window of his shotgun house into a new life of independence with a vehemently thirsty slate to quench.

Matt attended one semester at Missouri State University and flunked out. He started reading Kerouac, drinking whiskey, having unexceptional sex, and six months after he left his dogmatic adolescence, he hitchhiked to Alaska with a plan to jump on a fishing boat and head to sea.

Bright-eyed and incurably grinning with the novelty of new places and people, Matt fell in love with a punk rock Yupik girl that he met in the southeast port town of Cordova. He was reeling in his newfound life and riding a wave of inspiration that he couldn't help but to see glowingly transparent in everything he looked at. He grew his hair out long and greasy and began wearing a ponytail and then later two pigtails with a dirty bandana wrapped around his head. He tried to instill ruggedness onto his face with an abusive amount of two-dollar Top tobacco and cheap plastic whiskey bottles, but the baby bright skin and puerile look in his eye could shine through even the dishevelment of a three-week razorless, bathless, sea sweating halibut hunt.

Matt followed his wild Yupik love affair north to Fairbanks where he found himself amid a community of crazed writers and hallucinating musicians. He immediately began settling into a two-year stint of workshop words and custodial employment. Even the mop happy shit paste he cleaned off university toilets gave Matthew a sense of accomplishment and an intoxicating appetite to write and read and revel in the company of new friends and ideals.

That year Matt had his first birthday party. It was ridiculously large and complete with pony kegs, marijuana cake, and a live band. He drank himself into the cold Alaskan bonfire night until the sun never came up in the morning. Feral northern lights howled overhead in a cosmic dance and brilliant words like poetry dripped out of Matt's eager mouth and drenched everyone he touched with fraternal delight.

Matt was home, Matt was happy. He danced with long and clumsy limbs to the hepness of everyone around him. He inspired us all and gave birth to the possibility of a newborn man with the mission to never sell himself back to the stagnancy of an indolent life or god. He wrote about his family, his estranged jehovah culture and wrote so well that the phonetic flow born from his pen inspired descriptions and prose somewhere between Twain and Bukowski that Jack himself would have clapped his hands to hear.

And then one morning Wendy left him in his Notforeverland, the writing group split up and out and Fairbanks grew cold with unfamiliar faces, so Matt packed up his new life and lore and instead of going anywhere else in the vastness of the unabridged world, he headed back to Springfield, misery. He tried to keep his mentality alive on napkin scribbles at the back tables of barren bars, but a reunion with his mama, a boring new girlfriend, and the monotonous work of starting a twelve-hour-day roofing business left him dry and lackadaisical. Matthew began to grow callous and old and forget how to make his pen sing. And so it stopped and saddened and now wordless years have cowered by him and I wonder upon the unrecognizable sound of his voice on an incurious cell phone whether there exists a switch somewhere that has the power to turn on and off a human being—erasing memories, promises, and prose.

Nicholas Michael Ravnikar

Paradise Is Not an Option, but We'll Take What We Can Get

Turning the radio dial released a stream of coffee from the spout below the dash. A thin cloud of steam danced upward, and he thought of cardboards and steel drums and other important things. Employees in pale blue shirts each walked from their cars, adjusting name tags and reaching into oversized pockets for a jumble of keys to unlock the door, turn by heavy turn.

We have run from the world to this place. We obsess our dispensations. We are cold from choosing, and we are late for work.

Life on Earth occasionally makes one feel quite small.

The effects of this sensation can have tremendous repercussions.

Take this man, whom we shall call Gaston.

He now stands beneath a middle-aged tree, draping his arms in sheets of slick brown tape. He has wound the strips of film about him and lets them sway in the breeze. In his eyes, a deeply rooted desire somehow finds fulfillment. His mouth corked with an apple, his eyes incredibly difficult to see: he, Gaston, has invented a culture in which we may consider being an unequivocal participant.

His is the relatively simple solution.

No one could expect how the sun might feel for a person unaware of their own age, wearing a hat patched together from scraps of their whole life's wardrobe's thin fabrics. Except him. And beneath his hat, the range of bleached quills that would stand up straight whenever he wanted. His car horn blared the opening strains of a hit song by James Brown whenever he punched the wheel. Yes, a born winner.

Satisfaction, surely, the most difficult thing to achieve. Without that, all of life quite meaningless. Weeds and rubble around the building. His mother born here.

Go ahead. Watch.

If they call his name from the roof, he will refuse to answer them, for they are too careful with their money.

She should have walked out of the kitchen as soon as he looked down at his book and started reading, he thought. But it was too late now. Obviously an argument would come of it either way.

There should have been less light, more humor, no discussion. Everything would be different then, everything.

I should sell all of my possessions and go on drifting, too, he remembered thinking. I should make a solid attempt at learning five new languages. Maybe just one would be nice. Then I could translate for foreigners.

Instead he just goes on standing there, dark tape flapping from his body, otherwise naked but for the patchwork hat, arms raised in a T beneath the green, green leaves of a middle-aged tree, enjoying the summer sun and the way it warms him so.

Dawn Sueoka
Journey to the Moon »

The scientists, old men whose rickety faces seemed as strenuous and foul as the hull of a ship, were surprised to find, upon arriving on the moon, large colonies of wasps.

There were exactly nine hundred eighty seven million, six hundred fifty four thousand, three hundred twenty one of them.

Their long legs swept slowly back and forth as they moved through the air, like delicate oars drawing a little skiff across the water. Their larvae, encased by an oaky secretion, hung, as if suspended by threads, three to four feet above the lunar surface. The twitching larvae caused the pods to jostle each other gently.

The scientists felt blessed. They rushed back and forth, the ashy lunar dust that dappled their faces leaping up as they moved, and then settling again into the folds of their robes and the brittle moss of their beards. To the valleys and poles they traveled, in carriages of gauze. They scooped up torrents of wasps in great white nets and plucked the warbling pods from the air.

They returned to the ship with a dazzling chorus of data.

"Incredible!" they whispered as they fastened microscopic banners to edges of the wasps' legs then plunged two-inch pins through their bluish exoskeletons and creamy insides. The scientists thought of heaven, and of chocolate-coated candies as they signed their names in pen.

Living on the moon, the wasps had lost their stingers.

But the most amazing discovery was that the wasps had also shed their wings: tiny veined flakes littered the entire surface of the moon and made it appear from Earth vast and arctic, like the illuminated lens of a distant microscope.

Sally Reno

The Light from a Sports Bar a Thousand Miles Away

Saturday afternoon, Michael calls from Gainesville. It's very loud all around him.

I can't hear him clearly.

"Where are you?" I ask.

He seems to say he's in a sports bar, about to watch a prizefight. I add this up: Michael has had no alcohol, no cigarette, no illicit drug, and very little illicit sex since September 14, 1989.

"You're where?" I ask. It seems so incongruous.

"I'm in hell," he says, "hoping you might want to join me here."

"I'm on the balcony. I could jump and be there with you shortly," I offer.

He sighs, "That would be very nice." He says this very sweetly and I can hear him clearly now.

Bobbie Louise Hawkins
Nudists Walk on Coals >>

It's like feet are on top of the list when fools get creative. Did you see in the paper that seven nudists were taken to a hospital emergency room with severely burned feet? They decided to walk on hot coals and they did it.

Was it a dare? Did one of those people no one should ever listen to come up with a suggestion?

Picture it... It's night and we've got nudists around a campfire, dodging sparks. They're not there for a "let's all get nekkid" orgy. They've done everything wholesome nakedness allows. Roasted marshmallows. Sung songs. They're bored. All they've got is themselves, mosquitoes, and a bed of coals. And, "Hey! I've got an idea!"

Was that all it took?

Or did they deliberately prepare a bed of coals, the company gathered and waiting; a lot of naked bodies and an idea.

Then, when they launched, what was the format?

Did they all do it at once; walk onto the coals in a mob, and go mob-screaming to the other side?

It's hard to think they went one at a time, each one running screaming the length of the coal bed, and the next ones waiting for it to be their turn.

Was number seven seven times dumber than number one?

If it was a bet were there winners who walked on

coals and didn't end up in the Emergency Room?

To go to the hospital, did the drivers get dressed? Did the victims get dressed as well, minus shoes of course?

Two cars drive up to the Emergency Room Entrance at the Hospital.

The nudists enter. And then what?

Nurses have forms to fill out, questions to ask.

"How did this happen?" and the admitting nurse, pen in hand, waits for the answer.

Leah Rogin-Roper
Two Truths and a Lie >>

When I was little, my sisters and I used to dress our black cat, Bella, up in baby clothes. She was a gentle cat and would stare at me with deep green eyes as we crammed her legs into the frilly pink dress and tied the matching bonnet tightly around her chin. One day we lowered Bella into the pool to see if she could swim. I'm not sure how she made it back out.

I don't like Richard Brautigan, Virginia Woolf, or Hunter S. Thompson.

Sometimes I lie when the truth would serve me better.

>>

I think people who commit suicide are rude and selfish.

I saw a dead homeless woman on the street in San Francisco as I walked by one morning on my way to work. Her lips were grey and there were already several people around her. Even though I am certified in first aid and CPR, I didn't stop to see if there was anything I could do.

My parents were hippies. I usually lie and say they were lawyers with social consciences. I gloss over the commune, the vegan Thanksgivings, the silent Fourths of July.

>>

Once on a summer day in Virginia, I lounged in the air-conditioned house, completely ignoring the fact that my dogs were out in the hot sun with no water. When my mom came home and noticed, she dragged me outside by my hair and locked me in the dog pen. I huddled together with the panting dogs in the slight shade of their house.

Although my parents did a lot of drugs, I never held it against them.

When they called to tell me about my mother, for a frozen moment I almost laughed.

>>

When I was in high school I used to get really stoned before softball games. My teammates were a slew of southern belles who did their hair and makeup intricately and loudly before each game. Once they tried to have a team prayer before the game, but I looked the other girls in the eye, smirked, and walked out.

When people told me they'd put my mother in their prayers, there was a snide voice inside me that said, "Yeah, you do that."

I don't trust male gynecologists.

>>

I've never finished an entire Ernest Hemingway novel and I probably never will.

When I was fifteen, I got drunk at a party and made

out with my older cousin. I still don't know whose fault it was.

The last time I spoke to my mother on the phone, I hung up on her.

>>

I haven't been inside a church during a sermon for at least twenty years and I'm not even thirty yet.

I was a teenager the first and only time I ever pulled a hit and run. I came around a corner too fast and skidded into someone's car. I still remember meeting my friend John's eyes and the look in them as I put the car in reverse.

I thought about suicide a lot when I was a kid. Mostly I pictured the pained look on my parents' faces as they mourned over my tragically small body.

>>

In elementary school, I shoplifted Sweet Valley High books. My mother called them trash and refused to buy them for me. I had an allowance and could have bought them for myself, but they were more fun to steal. I also used to steal purple eye-liner that I was not allowed to wear. I never got caught.

I don't like to talk on the phone and almost never answer it.

The last morning I saw my mom alive I was relieved to open up the door and send her away.

>>

I've tried every drug that doesn't have to be injected. The only one I like is pot, but I also keep myself well-stocked with prescription pharmaceuticals.

I've read the journals of anyone who ever left them within my reach.

Once I was babysitting for a two-year-old and I passed out on the couch. When I woke up he was gone. For that split second of terror I could see the horror of finding him, finger dangling limply from the electric socket, head submerged in the toilet. For a moment I imagined the rest of my life as the babysitter who let something happen. The door hung slightly open, and I quickly walked out of it. He was sitting on the front porch swing, staring longingly off into the distance.

>>

Some days I can't remember the sound of my mom's voice.

She might have called and I might not have answered.

Occasionally I'll put my own baby down for a nap before she's really tired just so I can get some time to write.

>>

I minored in Spanish but I can't really speak it. When I studied in Chile, I told the host family I lived with that I was allergic to mayonnaise because they liked to put it on everything and I think it's gross.

I've slept with every single one of my brother's

best friends.

I'm not sure if she took the pills from me or not.

>>

Sometimes I buy vegetables, like the dark shriveled eggplant I just disposed of, knowing I'll never cook them and that I'll end up throwing them away.

I can't remember the last thing I said to my mother.

I like to read children's books in the bathtub. I must have read A Little Princess at least one hundred times. It doesn't make me cry.

Every store is closed. That is good. It is hidad. The streets are deserted. Good, good, as it should be. Proper. I hold my head with one hand. The sun is too bright and the silence hurts, in a way nothing else has, yet. There should be the din of children talking, shouting, laughing; taxi drivers arguing, smoking, bored, shouting over and over again to take people to the checkpoint at Ram. Even the roosters, it seems, have refused to acknowledge the sunrise. I cannot remember hearing them. Not since they came to us with the news.

My chest aches for the silence to be broken by what passes for normal.

There is rubbish in the gutters as usual: crumpled cigarette packs, empty pop bottles, bits of newspaper, the ubiquitous black plastic bag. I hate this. I hate this. When did we lose our pride? This is still our country; we treat her like she's already lost. Perhaps she is. I am a fool. Of course she is.

But the stones are still here, in the street, smashed where they fell. At the feet of whom we still aren't clear. Different reports. The news, the neighbors, the teachers all say different things. Soldiers. Settlers. What does it matter now?

Muntasir's grandfather ignores the stones, steps carefully through the charred metal and rubber remains of a tire. He rings the bell. There is no need. The gate has been kicked off its hinges, but he is a proper old man. It is still a school after all.

I never liked the principal. He is kind today, though. Full of sorrow and honoring words for Muntasir. Upstairs classroom, he says, gesturing. It's the largest. The old man nods. The classroom, I remember from my own days at the school, is not that big. The men of the village will have to come and sit with the family in turns, a few at a time, but they'll understand. They will be patient. Every boy and man in El Bireh knows the routine.

The principal offers to make the bitter coffee. That is good. The old man nods.

I breathe deeply, when I remember to breathe, and it occurs to me that the schoolyard smells like promises. Pine and rose fill my senses, but there's more to it than that. Everything is brighter than I remember, from the last time I was here, to speak to Muntasir's teachers just two weeks before. Too bright, and suddenly, too loud. Birds sing overhead. The fountain near the entrance giggles like a daughter.

In the early morning sun, the building appears to be on fire. I know the stone of this building like the contours of my wife's body, the smell of her breath. Jerusalem stone. It is everywhere. The building, the driveway, the steps, the path. It is a thing apart, alive, lit from the inside. It changes constantly, like a mood, is no one color for more than an instant—not ivory, not gold, not even a single shade of red: carnelian, ruby, fresh blood, dried blood.

Except for that spot over there. And the one next to it.

The principal follows my gaze and screams for the

custodian. Abu Suleiman's thin, bony frame flutters out nervously from the building like a zaghlool, the tiny bird Muntasir's mother cooked for his birthday dinner four days ago. He has a bucket in one hand and a sponge in the other.

I wonder what he hopes to accomplish. There isn't enough soap and water in the world to wash my son's blood from these stones.

K. Scott Forman
Mercy >>

Autumn had not changed the mountain pass. It still appeared as it did when I had been a boy hunting deer with my father. The colors were the same yellows, oranges, and reds, the air still chilled with the hint of wood smoke, the ground covered with dying leaves and grasses mingled with rocks and twigs, damp and soft to the boot. Snow had fallen at the higher elevations, and the cold of snow worked its way with the wind through my clothing and into my bones.

The earth, musty and mulch-ridden, was slowly hiding the life of the previous spring and would combine with fall's leaves to bring life back in the spring. The smell of the leaves and grass, the other dead things, decaying in the fall foliage combined with the cold wood-smoke air into a perfume: slightly unpleasant, yet inviting. I was alone, more alone than I had ever been.

There wasn't that much blood. A lot less than when my father would clean and dress out a deer. I had helped many times in the past as a boy, but this was the first time I had to actually do the task by myself. I missed my father. The work was strange in its familiarity, the heat of the blood brought memories, the smell of life ebbing away with the metallic bullet and gunpowder, but there was a hole in my soul that I had not anticipated. I had never pulled the trigger. I had never been the killer. I had never felt guilt.

I dug the hole deep into the forest floor to keep

scavengers away. Although a cougar, or coyote, or even a bear would only digest what remained, I did what I had been taught. It was a tradition, a habit learned long ago, and it was part of me.

The carcass would hang in a cheesecloth bag keeping what remained of the flying bugs off the meat. Any other time it would be a day or two, and then we would cut and wrap the larger pieces, jerk the rest. There would be no extra days this time. This part of the hunt had always been my favorite, lounging around camp, looking at the carcasses, cooking some of the kill, slicing some of the meat thin to jerk; I believe the evidence of life draining to the ground, and having in some way been responsible for extinguishing that life, sustained me, made me feel powerful, safe, even self-sufficient. This time I felt powerless, helpless.

Beer was the drink of choice on these trips, and my father had allowed me to drink as much as I wanted from the age of twelve. Beer was something I wished I had with me now, but there hadn't been time. I had to get it done and get on with my life.

I dreamed about it the first night. It wasn't so much the look of the blood, but the smell of the earth mingled with the blood; I awoke smelling a death that had not occurred. It was clear that it had been a painless death, and probably too long in coming.

He didn't struggle. We walked, and he had tried to keep going as I followed. I lost him once, and when I found him in the brush, exhausted, lost, that was the moment I started feeling guilty. I put a bullet through his skull, lifted him onto my shoulders, and carried him back to camp. It took all of half a day.

The dead crackle under the weight of boots, a harsh sound that is quickly softened by damp autumn ground beneath, scares anything living away, or at least alerts things nearby. The dead lay with the dead, nourishing the living that lay above. Soon, in months, this place would be alive, flowers budding, grass growing, trees pregnant with green waiting to burst forth. For now, Death stalked these woods, and Death had found His prey. He had brought my father here, followed him, and did the job.

The trail led to this place, his body a few yards from the bend. Life was a trail that led to many places, some living, some dying, but none walking the fence between life and death. Soon, what remained of the autumn life would join the rest in a colorful death, the remains sleeping until spring only to be reborn. He would not be coming back in the spring; he would not be reborn.

"Is that you, honey?" My wife called when I returned.

"Yes."

She had always been there for me, always been my support.

"Are you alright?"

"Yeah, I'll be fine."

"I know it's something you didn't want to do," she said, "but he wanted it this way."

"I know, I know." I had no words to express my feelings. "I miss him."

Somewhere in my churning brain and aching heart I felt bells ringing.

"Hey Dad, the police are on the phone. Do you think they've found Grandpa?"

"Hello."

The police reported the same thing they had for several days now.

"Yes. Yes. I understand." I hung up the phone and felt drained of all energy. My wife took my hand.

"What did they say?"

"They said that with my father's dementia, combined with the time he has been missing, the weather, and his age... They're not holding out much hope."

My wife began to cry. She wasn't sad. My father was in a better place.

It is night and if it was day you would see that everything is dry and covered with dust, you would see that it was not a flood that ripped through the narrow Palestinian street, sweeping everything askew so that to glimpse a right angle would startle you. Where there are still faded blue shutters on the buildings, they hang from only one hinge, every one hanging that way, as though a common style. It is night and in the darkness that is total because the electricity is out, Layla imagines that the dark that clings to the facades, to the debris she dodges with each step, is mud covering everything, that it was a flood that shook all these buildings and lives from their foundations. A flood is cleaner than the bombs, those evil hot flashes, the pungent smoke that is shot into the mortar of the buildings remaining there, reminding you of the human power that imagined those bombs into those streets. A marking and claiming and indifferent kind of smell.

Tonight the street is deserted—her battalion has made sure of that—but it is not silent. In the distance there is the faint thrumming of a diesel engine. She follows this sound a couple of minutes, almost tripping on the debris in the road. A flashlight forbidden, just in case.

She comes to the fifth doorway on her right. The door is open and the blackness that fills it taunts her, moves out at her and draws back at the same time. She doesn't mind the challenge and moves into it slowly as if into water, all her senses inflamed, registering the quality of that blackness. A few steps in and she pauses. There is a mistake, there is the smell of blood, of diesel fumes, but there is no smell of shit. He is still alive. She is curious, and welcomes the warmth of this new emotion into the dead steel trance of her duty. A particle of her flows back into her, is awakened. A tiny ember she thought was extinguished years ago and miles away from here.

Inside, the thrumming of the machine is louder and its tone higher. She removes her shoes, takes five paces down the hallway. On the fifth pace she pauses, her right foot senses the sliver of absence between the floor and the trap door beneath the short rug. She stands there for a moment imagining that it feels warmer there. There is something comforting about the rhythmic tremor beneath her foot, something that for a moment makes her forget why she is here. She slides her foot further along the carpet and finds its edge, uses her toes to roll it back towards her. There is not latch nor handle nor strap to pull the hatch up with, so she fits her slender fingers into two corners of the panel and pulls with all her strength. For a moment she and the hatch are at stasis. Then it gives. It is heavy, a single board, four inches thick, milled from the type and size of a tree that is only myth now.

Sound spills out and the smell of blood too. Then the diesel fumes, heavier and slower than the rest. There is no ladder, only a rope to descend by. It is blacker than black down there. She fits her headlamp over her knit cap, drops her bag of cosmetics into the black and does not hear it land for the din of the machine. A short way down the rope she switches on the headlamp but does not look towards the machine. She knows he is still alive, can feel him there, can feel too that he is beyond the sharp-edged pleading of pain, beyond pain as most humans know and should ever have to know it. In this being there is something worse than suffering. There is complete resignation. Pain has taken over and all the hope, hidden and apparent, that sustains life is gone.

She gathers her bag and rises. The white LED halo sprays against the source of the noise.

His face is a blur that will not come into focus. His face is a blur that will not come into focus. His face will not come into focus.

His face is strapped to the side of the diesel generator with two bicycle inner tubes. She would leave him there out of focus if she could, but she has orders. She switches the machine off and stares at him. He still does not look like a man.

The being emits a raspy air, barely more than breath itself. His sound gets louder, testing syllables. Nonsense she thinks until there is a pattern that she would not hear but for the total silence, the total dark. Arabic.

Don't leave me here alone.

She wants to kill him. Not from hate or duty or patriotism or madness, but because she feels nothing. Nothing moves in her, and she sees herself there, dead. She sits and cannot cry cannot speak. Somehow my breath is still taking, still giving, why?

She will not paint this one, will not perforate the

clotted tissue, will not place skull pieces back beneath skin and comb the matter out of hair, will not cleanse death to exonerate the living. She will not photograph this one or any other. No one will get away with it with her help ever again.

Sitting, his head in her lap, the warmth of his blood soaks into her, kindling the spark that flew into her amidst all that absence.

He begins to speak as he dies.

When I was a child there were olive trees...

Layla can see them, she will always remember them for him.

Benjamin Dancer
Elaine >>

I met Elaine a few months after her death. I was newly married and obsessed with a mountain lion of which I had grown fond. I had spent several years poking around his dens, examining his scat and dissecting his kills. I carried a can of mace in my pocket against the eventuality that my invasive curiosity might provoke him to violence, but it would not come as a surprise if, from his point of view, having me around was akin to having food in the pantry. I thought, at first, Elaine was one of his kills. It was summer. When the scent of her decomposition was carried up through the ponderosa forest on the breeze, I immediately began zigzagging down the mountain.

On my first zig I found the left shoulder strap of Elaine's Fruit of the Loom bra snagged on a barkless log. On the following zag I found her panties under the stem of a flowering rose—then her silver plastic bracelet under the outer edge of a juniper bush, followed by one of her plastic jeweled earrings in the leaves of a kinnikinnick patch. Two hundred feet into my descent I found Elaine.

The first thing I did was talk to her. It was clear to me that she died violently and that the lion had nothing to do with her death. As I spoke, I hesitated before I used the word; nevertheless, I did use it. I committed to do everything in my power to bring her justice. By the time I uttered the phrase, though, I no longer believed in justice and began to grieve. I sat beside her and stroked her hair. The ponderosas were aromatic, but the pungency of Elaine's decay was overwhelming. The scent of her death was fundamentally different than the death I was accustomed to in the forest, and in this respect the experience was alien to me.

As I sat and looked into her empty eye sockets, I saw her murder as a violation of a relationship. Her brain had liquified and oozed into the pine needles long before my arrival. A beetle scampered out of her skinless mouth and under her jaw to crawl back up and across her lower molars. Others were feeding on the black stain at my feet, the desiccated remains of her liquified brain.

As I talked to her it did not seem to me like justice could be imposed. I was certain of this, perhaps: justice was not something I, nor anybody else, could execute against another person. Coyotes, it appeared, had entered her carcass through her anus and in the process of penetrating her sacrum to reach her intestines, they strewed her right leg over a decomposing log where they and other scavengers devoured the muscles of that leg.

I realized that justice is either unattainable or voluntary and was bewildered by this and began to think of my own father. Some disappointments are permanent. Her abdomen and chest, apart from the desiccation of her skin, appeared to be intact. I imagined the violence that ended her life, what it was like for her to die, and grieving for her loneliness, I posed a question to Elaine hardly expecting an answer: what is justice if not the restoration of relationship?

Elaine only replied that she could not be restored. Which was so obvious when I looked again at her naked corpse, I felt embarrassed for asking the question. Her leg bones were completely exposed from the head of both femurs down to where the skin of her feet was ragged around the base of both tibias and fibulas.

The mothers of those beetles carefully laid their eggs in Elaine's putrescent flesh. The baby beetles hatched and began to eat Elaine. They had been eating her all of their lives.

The most shocking sight on Elaine's carcass was her hair, how beautiful it was. I realized as I stroked her hair that I was uncertain which measure of my grief was for her and which was for myself. Maybe truth exists, a conviction. You killed Elaine; it is known. But how can that conviction, a jail sentence, an execution help her now?

There exist relationships irreparable, living deaths as putrid and fecund as her corpse. Like father and son. Nevertheless, I committed myself to a dead woman and saw with my own eyes that death is a feast. It did not take long for the bacteria in Elaine's digestive track to thrive on her very tissue. Within days the gas from their excretions bloated her corpse. Those chemicals were eventually carried up through the ponderosa forest to my lungs where matter that once constituted Elaine was absorbed into my bloodstream.

There are simple truths. Elaine ate to live. Whether she harvested the food herself or purchased it from a grocer, each meal required the consumption or, if you will, the death of plants and animals. Now bacteria, coyotes, beetles and a host of other organisms are converting her nutrition into a form the grass can absorb.

I have seen force—I believe in the power of the beetle's jaw. I have seen that death is also life, and I am no longer able to draw acute distinctions between the two states of being.

Acknowledgments >>

Our first collection would not have been possible without the time and dedication of many people. We thank Leah Rogin-Roper for her conception, vision, leadership, and dedication to this project.

Acknowledged, too, is the Editorial Board for taking the time to read through a multitude of submissions and for supplying their editorial knowledge, the second tier of readers for offering their input during the submission process, the copy editors for their thorough examination and research of the final manuscript, and finally, the Design Board for their time and expertise with the cover and layout.

We would also like to offer a special acknowledgment to Barbara Henning and Andrew Wille for taking the time to examine the manuscript and offer their editorial advice.

Of course, none of this would be possible without the talented contributions of the writers themselves. Hold fast, and keep moving forward.

Lastly, thank you, reader, for taking the time to indulge in our first edition of fast forward.

For further information about FF>>, please contact the Editorial Board at: editorff@gmail.com, or visit our website:

www.fastforwardpress.wordpress.com

About the Authors >>

Megan Burns has been most recently published in *Callaloo*, *Constance Magazine* and *Exquisite Corpse*. She lives in New Orleans where she and her husband, poet Dave Brinks, run the 17 Poets! reading series. Her book *Memorial + Sight Lines* is forthcoming from Lavender Ink (May 2008).

Benjamin Dancer is a writer, and he teaches the humanities at Jefferson County Open School in Lakewood, Colorado.

Linh Dinh is the author of two collections of stories, *Fake House* (Seven Stories Press 2000) and *Blood and Soap* (Seven Stories Press 2004), four books of poems, *All Around What Empties Out* (Tinfish 2003), *American Tatts* (Chax 2005), *Borderless Bodies* (Factory School 2006), and *Jam Alerts* (Chax 2007), with a novel, *Love Like Hate*, scheduled to be released in 2008 by Seven Stories Press. His work has been anthologized in *Best American Poetry 2000*, *Best American Poetry 2004*, *Best American Poetry 2007*, and *Great American Prose Poems from Poe to the Present*, among other places. Linh Dinh is also the editor of the anthologies *Night, Again: Contemporary Fiction from Vietnam* (Seven Stories Press 1996) and *Three Vietnamese Poets* (Tinfish 2001), and translator of *Night, Fish and Charlie Parker*, the poetry of Phan Nhien Hao (Tupelo 2006). *Blood and Soap* was chosen by the Village Voice as one of the best books of 2004. His poems and stories have been translated into Italian, Spanish, Dutch, German, French, Portuguese, Japanese, Arabic, and Icelandic. He has also published widely in Vietnamese.

K. Scott Forman teaches writing at Weber State University in Utah, loves long walks on deserted Afghan beaches, sunsets, and the letter X. He is happily married with children and hopes to be a writer when he grows up.

Bobbie Louise Hawkins was raised in West Texas, studied art in London, taught in missionary schools in British Honduras, attended a Jesuit University in Tokyo while acting on radio and the stage, and had her first one-woman show of paintings and collages in New York at the Gotham Book Mart Gallery in 1969. In 1979 she was one of 100 writers from eleven countries attending the "One World Poetry" festival in Amsterdam and was awarded Fellowship in Literature by the National Endowment for the Arts. She has published 18 books of both prose and poetry. Her most recent book, *Absolutely Eden*, will be published by United Artists in June 2008. At Anne Waldman's invitation she began the prose concentration of study at Naropa University, where she continues to teach.

Barbara Henning is the author of two novels and six books of poetry. Recent poems and stories have been published in *The Brooklyn Rail, Zen Monster, Jacket Magazine, Slavery: Cyberpoems, Talisman, Reconfigurations, Not Enough Night* and *Eoagh*. Professor Emerita at Long Island University, she now teaches for Naropa

University and University of Arizona's Poetry Center.

Bryan Jansing was born in Charleston, South Carolina on December 31, 1971 and was raised in Italy. "Grand Love" was published in *Parole in Corsa III* 2005 (Full Color Sound), "Cold Feet" was a finalist for *Glimmer Train* (2006) and he has been published in *Arkansas Valley Journal, INsite Magazine,* and *Women's Business Chronicle.* He currently lives in Denver, Colorado where he's ghost writing the memoirs of Ron Gonen, an international thief living somewhere in the U.S. in hiding from the Israeli Mafia.

Kaen Joyler is the editor of *agora journal.* Recent work has appeared in *The Abacot Jourrnal* and Fret Punch Press's *Corpse of Milk.* He teaches EFL in Seoul, South Korea, where he's been flying under radar for the past decade.

Elizabeth Keicher is a poet and short story writer from Buffalo, New York. She is pursuing her MFA in Creative Writing at Naropa University and is currently starting up Rubied Press, a publishing venture that features Buffalo writers and artists. Most recently her poems will appear in *Streams of Unconsciousness.*

Justin M. Kulyk is a novel writer from Raleigh, North Carolina. He lives in New Albany, Ohio, and is in the MFA Program for Creative Writing through Naropa University (projected completion 2009). Kulyk is currently constructing a novel in the Apollonian school of style. His works have been published in *Fear Knocks* and *Monkey Puzzle* (Issue 3).

Liam McAuliffe lives the good life on the far north coast of California. He is currently working on his first novel.

Kona Morris has been writing flash fiction since she was a child but has only started calling it such within the last year when she finally understood "flash fiction" to mean, "really short shot glasses full of one hundred proof literature." More bang per ounce. Patrón. She is on the Editorial Board for *fast forward* (FF>>), and she was co-founder of the Write Trash writing group in Fairbanks, Alaska. She received the Redwood Empire Mensa Award for Creative Non-Fiction in 2006, and her work has most recently been published in *Toyon*, *Be Brave Bold Robot*, and *The Bathroom*.

Val D. Phillips, together with her partner, family and friends, is co-creating a rural intentional community in Gardner, Colorado committed to social justice, sustainability and shared spiritual practice. She lived and worked in Palestine from 1992-1994, returning to the region in 2001 with the International Solidarity Movement engaging in non-violent direct action aimed at ending the illegal Israeli military and civilian occupation of the West Bank and Gaza.

Nicholas Michael Ravnikar is Nicholas Michael Ravnikar.

Sally Reno is The Mad Hatter, tea sommelier at large and a founder of The Green Tea   Party. She is a newscaster and reporter for KGNU community radio, where she also writes and produces news and features. Ms. Reno has been assistant to the Mayor of NYC, a writer/editor for the NYC Planning Commission and was chief public information officer for Tucson Water, the public utility. Like Senator Obama, Ms. Reno keeps in touch with former leaders of the Weather Underground. Her first novel has been out of print for a long time.

Leah Rogin-Roper lives in the mountains of Colorado. Her work has appeared in various publications, including *Mountain Gazette*, *Powder Magazine*, and *Pathfinder*. She teaches at Red Rocks Community College.

Nancy Stohlman is a Denver writer, international human rights worker, and the co-author and -editor of *Live From Palestine* (South End Press), which was nominated for a Colorado Book Award. She has been published in *Counterpunch.com*, *Commondreams.com*, *Resist*, *The Bloomsbury Review*, *Snowline Poetry Journal*, and she is a contributing author to the book *Peace Under Fire* (Verso). Stohlman is co-founder of Whole World Press, a progressive publishing company that launched in 2008.

Dawn Sueoka is from Honolulu, Hawai'i. She is currently in Naropa University's low-residency MFA program. She lives in Ann Arbor, Michigan.

Stacy Walsh grew up in Michigan and currently works and resides in Los Angeles. She is working on a collection of short stories detailing her experiences in the film industry and is nearing completion of her MFA in Creative Writing from Naropa University.

Andrew Wille lives west of London. He is a teacher of creative writing and an editor, and his fiction and nonfiction have appeared in *American Drivel Review*, *Bombay Gin*, *The Cafe Irreal*, *Ellipsis*, *One Less*, and *Uncontained*.

FF>>

This book is set in Helvetica Neu *and* Garamond *typefaces. It was designed in Racine, WI and printed in Minneapolis, MN by BookMobile in an edition of 401.*